THE GRASSHOPPER AND THE ANTS

Reading Consultant: Prue Goodwin, Lecturer in literacy and children's books

ORCHARD BOOKS
338 Euston Road, London NW1 3BH
Orchard Books Australia
Level 17/207 Kent Street, Sydney, NSW 2000

First published in 2011
First paperback publication in 2012

ISBN 978 1 40830 966 7 (hardback)
ISBN 978 1 40830 974 2 (paperback)

A CIP catalogue record for this book is available
from the British Library.

1 3 5 7 9 10 8 6 4 2 (hardback)
1 3 5 7 9 10 8 6 4 2 (paperback)

Printed in Great Britain

Orchard Books is a division of Hachette Children's Books,
an Hachette UK company.

THE GRASSHOPPER AND THE ANTS

Written by Lou Kuenzler
Illustrated by Jill Newton

Old Aesop was an Ancient Greek –
his AWESOME FABLES are unique.
Each fun tale gives good advice
reminding us we must be nice.

Try very hard to share your toys
with other little girls and boys.
Write thank you notes for gifts you get.
Don't grab at things not given yet.
Listen well and use your wits,
unless you are a bunch of twits!

This fable warns you not to shirk
while other people do the work!

Working to a steady beat,
ants were gathering food to eat.
Up and down they marched all day –
never stopping off to play.

An idle grasshopper dozed nearby.
He shook his head and wondered why
the tiny ants were always busy.
All that marching made him dizzy!

This long-legged, dozing hippy
watched the ants and sang a ditty.
With an old guitar he played
while lying in a patch of shade:

Do-Be-Do-Be-Do-Be-Doo.
Why d'you find so much to do?
Why not spend your summer days
soaking up some sunny rays?

Do-Be-Do-Be-Do-Be-Doo.
A little rest is good for you.
Why not chill and sing some songs?
'Cos we could really get along.

Do-Be-Do-Be-Do-Be-Doo.
Enjoy the sun while skies are blue!

The busy ants just scuttled on –
Grasshopper laughed and sang his song.
He shared the tune with passing snails
who slowly spread their silver trails.

Grasshopper waved and said, "I'm Jim.
But all my friends just call me 'Slim'!"
He called the snails and gently strummed,
"Stop and rest, my slimy chums."

Do-Be-Do-Be-Do-Be-Doo!
I see you snails are busy too.
You really are so very slow.
Why not just rest – go with the flow!

"We're slow and steady!" said Snail One.
"It takes us time to get things done!"

"It really does," replied Snail Two.
"We're just so slow, we stick like glue!
I sometimes wish we had six feet . . .
they'd make the chores quick to complete."

“Chores are boring!” groaned Slim-Jim
“I’m out on strike! I won’t begin!”
He put his feet up on a sign
that said:
NO WORK IN SUMMERTIME!

He dozed and watched the butterflies
above him in the summer skies.

**Hey, pretty wings, just look at you,
flitting through the sky so blue!
I like the way you're having fun,
flying in the summer sun!**

**Do-Be-Do-Be-Do-Be-Doo.
Just do the things you like to do!**

The busy butterflies flew away:
"We've many eggs to lay today!"

A bee agreed: "It may be sunny,
but I must keep on making honey!"

A dung beetle was busy too,
rolling home a ball of poo.

"Of course I *need* to!" said the bug.
He gave the massive poop a hug.

This poo will feed me for a year.
You think it smells? Don't sit so near!

The busy creatures hurried on,
leaving Jim to sing his songs.
It seemed they all had things to do
while he found time to "Do-Bee-Doo!"

The tiny ants, most busy of all,
worked from dawn until nightfall.
All that month, they finished chores
as Slim Jim sang (and sometimes snored!).

They worked to fill their winter store.
Carrying more and more and more.
Day after day, they carried more,
pips and seeds and nuts galore.

We'll toil and work for all our clan,
following the Big Ant Plan.
We'll help each other to survive
and gather food to stay alive!
We'll work beneath the summer sun –
and be prepared when cold days come!

Grasshopper laughed and rolled his eyes.
He watched them lug their large supplies:

Do–Be–Do–Be–Do–Be–Doo.
I see you still have things to do.
Can't you rest just for one day?
Come and chill! Come sing and play!

"I'd love to stop, but there's no time!"
a girl ant said, the last in line.
"I have to carry home this seed.
I've hundreds of baby cousins to feed.
Our winter larder will stay empty
unless I work in times of plenty.
I'll gather food while the weather's fine
to store as lunch for wintertime."

"Winter?" laughed Grasshopper Jim –
her fussing seemed so odd to him!
"Winter is so far away.
Why worry on a summer's day?"

"Because I must!" came her reply,
"or else we will all starve and die."

"Wait up," said Jim. "So what's your
name?
You're so pretty, it's a shame
that you won't come and sit by me
beneath this dandelion tree.
And while the sun shines up above
I'll sing you songs of summer love!"

"My name's Antonia Ant," she said,
"but DON'T get ideas in your head!
You're NOT my type – you're FAR too
lazy –
a guy like you would drive me CRAZY!"

"But I can give you all you need!"
Jim offered her a fallen seed.

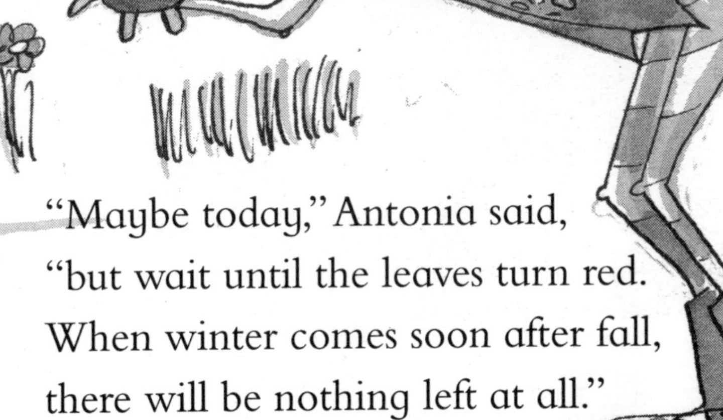

Ripe berries grow on every tree –
just look around and you will see.
There's food enough for me and you
AND any little cousins too.

"Maybe today," Antonia said,
"but wait until the leaves turn red.
When winter comes soon after fall,
there will be nothing left at all."

With that, she turned and marched
away,
leaving Jim to sing and play:

Dearest, sweet Antonia!
You're making me feel lonelier
than any guy should ever be!
Do-Be-Do-Be-Do-Be-Dee!
Won't you please come back to me?
Do-Be-Do-Be-Do-Be-Deeeeeee!

Of course, Antonia was quite right –
soon the sun was far less bright.
The leaves turned brown and bronze
and gold.
The nights turned long and very cold.

The summer butterflies had gone.
The snails hid with their warm shells on.

The bees had flown inside their hive –
they ate their honey to survive.

The dung beetle found a cosy spot . . .
Inside the poo it was steaming hot!

The ants were nowhere to be found –
they were living underground.

But hungry Jim was all alone.
He had no food – no winter home.

As he sang his sad voice quivered.
As he played his thin legs shivered.

Poor Jim grew slimmer every day
because he'd put no food away.
His skinny tum was TOTALLY empty.
He wished he'd saved in times of plenty.

Where summer grasses had once grown,
hay was cut. The field was mown.
Nothing showed but short, sharp stalks
along the tracks where Jimmy walked.

He staggered down the ants' old route
hoping for a leaf or shoot.
Alas, no morsel could be found –
no single seed dropped on the ground.

And then, of course, there came the
snow . . .
and Jim knew where he had to go.
He stumbled on, towards the sound
of marching feet from underground.

He squeezed inside an ant-sized door
and lay exhausted on the floor.

The ants had many mouths to feed –
the walls were lined with fruit and seeds.

Jim wheezed: "I know
you'll think me rude,
but – please – I need a little food!"

"Quick!" Antonia begged. "It's Jim! Hurry, ants! We must help him!"

But Queen Ant said, "Why should we
share?
Why should we help him? We don't care.
We worked hard while he was lazy,
then he dared to call *us* crazy!

He didn't store a scrap of food
because he wasn't 'in the mood'!
He didn't do a single thing
except to play guitar and sing!"

She told her soldiers, "Drag him away!"
But Antonia begged to let him stay.
"*Please*, Your Majesty, do one thing . . .
just listen to him play and sing."

"Oh, yes!" cried every small ant cousin.
"Let's hear a song – or half a dozen.
Although we've tons of food and rooms,
it's dull down here without his tunes . . ."

"He'll sing for food!" Antonia begged.
"If you like his songs, we'll share our bread."
"All right!" said Queen. "I'll hear him play . . .
and *if* I like it, he can stay!"

Jim staggered to his wobbly feet
and strummed a chord – a soulful beat.
He sang a gentle, lilting tune.
His music echoed around the room.

Now the summer sun is gone,
I have nothing but this song!
I've been a silly lazy twit
for never getting on with it!
My music's all I have to give.
Only songs can help me live.
I've been an empty-headed fool
for showing off and playing cool.

The room broke out in shouts and
cheers.
Antonia's eyes filled up with tears.

Queen Ant sighed, "I'll let him stay –
so long as I can hear him play!
We'll feed him till the start of spring
and in return he'll have to sing!"

The little ants all cried, "Hurrah!" –
Jim said he'd teach them all guitar.
He stayed on till the sun returned
and sang the moral he had learned:

Prepare yourself for days ahead
or else you might just end up dead!
Ants are really very wise
to think ahead to store supplies.
Do-Be-Do-Be-Do-Be-Doo.
I've learnt my lesson through and through!

Written by Lou Kuenzler
Illustrated by Jill Newton

The Hare and the Tortoise	978 1 40830 968 1
The Boy who cried Wolf	978 1 40830 969 8
The Town Mouse and the Country Mouse	978 1 40830 970 4
The Fox and the Stork	978 1 40830 971 1
The Lion and the Mouse	978 1 40830 972 8
The Goose that laid the Golden Eggs	978 1 40830 973 5
The Grasshopper and the Ants	978 1 40830 974 2
The Dad, the Boy and the Donkey	978 1 40830 975 9

All priced at £4.99

Orchard Books are available from all good bookshops, or can be ordered from our website, www.orchardbooks.co.uk, or telephone 01235 827702, or fax 01235 827703.